Psssst! It's Me . . . the Bogeyman

by Barbara Park

illustrated by Stephen Kroninger

An Anne Schwartz Book

ATHENEUM BOOKS FOR YOUNG READERS

To the genius who
invented the night-light.
My hero.
—B. P.

For Elaine,
Shoshonna, John,
and Yehuda
—S. K.

FIRST
EDITION

Atheneum Books for Young Readers
An imprint of Simon & Schuster Children's
Publishing Division
1230 Avenue of the Americas
New York, New York 10020

Text copyright © 1998 by Barbara Park
Illustrations copyright © 1998 by Stephen Kroninger

Book design by Ann Bobco
The text of this book is set in Univers.
The art for this book consists of collage
created from magazine photographs and cut paper.

First Edition
Printed in Singapore
10 9 8 7 6 5 4 3 2 1

Library of Congress Cataloging-in-Publication Data
Park, Barbara.
Pssst! It's Me . . . the Bogeyman / by Barbara Park ;
illustrated by Stephen Kroninger.—1st ed.
p.   cm.
"An Anne Schwartz book."
Summary: A genuine, creepy-crawly, blood-chilling,
spine-tingling Bogeyman, who lives under beds,
reveals something he soon regrets.
ISBN 0-689-81667-7
[1. Monsters—Fiction. 2. Fear—Fiction.]
I. Kroninger, Stephen, ill. II. Title.
PZ7.P2197Ps   1998
[E]—dc21   97-10123

Pssssssst!

Yo!

Down here . . . under the bed.

It's *me,*
the **Bogeyman.**

Yeah,

you heard me, Sparkie.

It's the GENUINE,

creepy-crawly,

BLOOD-CHILLING,

spine-tingling,

can't-avoid-the-urge-to-grab-your-ankle-

when-you're-climbing-into-the-sack,

Bogeyguy.

And the news doesn't get any better, Bud,
'cause I'm stew-spewin', gravel-chewin' mad.

Oh, quit your shivering, Skeezicks.
It isn't you who's got me fuming.
Here! Just take a look at this morning's headline!

THE NATIONAL SQUEALER

EVIL BOGEYMAN BELLOWS BOO

Boy Scouts Go Berserk

THE BOGEYMAN WILL GET YA IF YA DON'T WATCH OUT!

It's a lie, I tell you!

That lummox isn't me!

I don't go clomping after campers like some

bumbling, stumbling Frankenstein.

And even if I *did,*

I'd never stop and pose for pictures.

I'd lose my job, Jake.

Check it out. . . . It's all right here on page three of my Official Bogeyman Contract.

Official
Bogeyman Contract

The Bogeyman's identity must be protected at all costs.

No one must ever gaze upon your face,

or (heaven forbid!) take your picture

and then (perish the thought!) print it in the tabloids.

If any of these calamities should occur,

we, the management,

regret to inform you

that your services as the Bogeyman

will no longer be required.

There, see?
You've gotta help me clear my name!
The photo's a fake. A **fib.** A **fraud!**

And here's another NEWS FLASH, Filbert:

The Bogeyman doesn't say

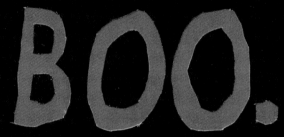

Boo's a baby word, Bubbie.

It rhymes with toodle-*loo*,

And Winnie the Pooh,

And it comes after *peek-a-*.

And right before *hoo*.

And okay, maybe if you scream it really loud

at a football game,

it might mean the ref made a bad call.

But no matter how you shout it,

boo just ain't scary, Skippy.

Want to know a *scary* word?
I'll give you five of 'em:

Go . . .

get . . .

ready . . .

for . . .

bed.

Yeah, you know what I'm talking about.
Especially if it's a dark and stormy night,
and your pj's are in your closet,
all the way in . . . the . . . back.
And oh, dearie me,
your lightbulb burned out last night.
But you fight your fear and head upstairs.

Then you stop at the top and peer

into the pitch-black darkness of your room.

You'd have to be insane to go in there.

Am I right, Dwight?

But suddenly, your dim-witted feet rush you right

across your rug,

and deposit you slap dab in front of your closet door

which swings open *all by itself*.

(Hmm. That's odd.)

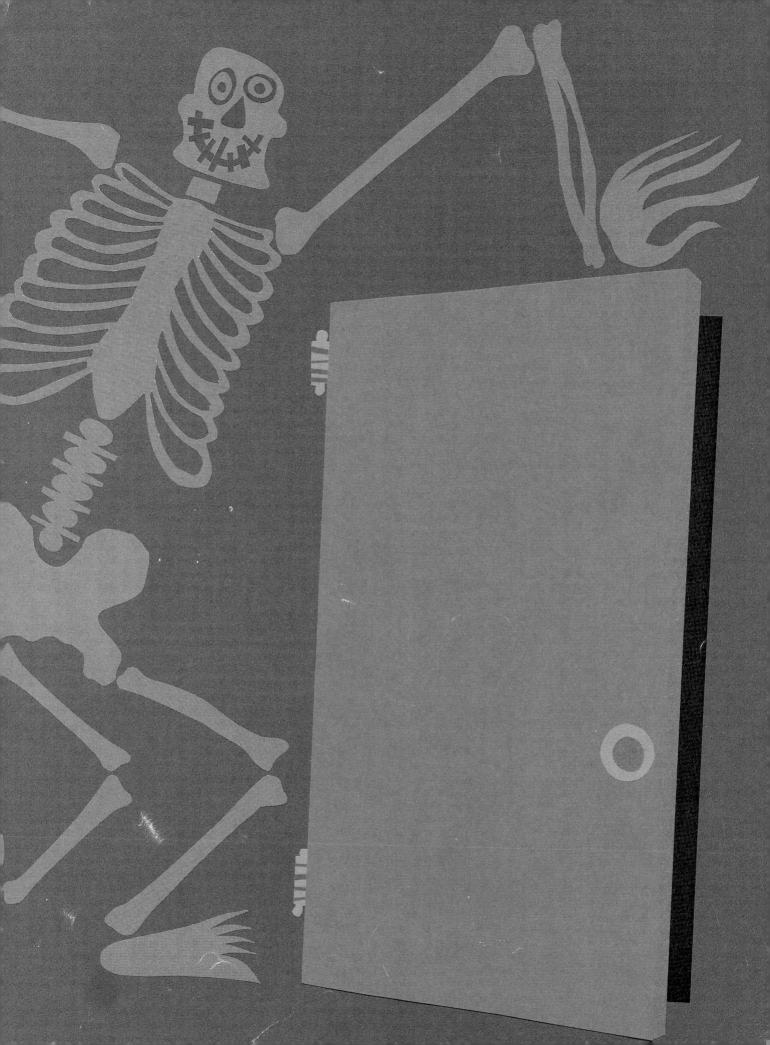

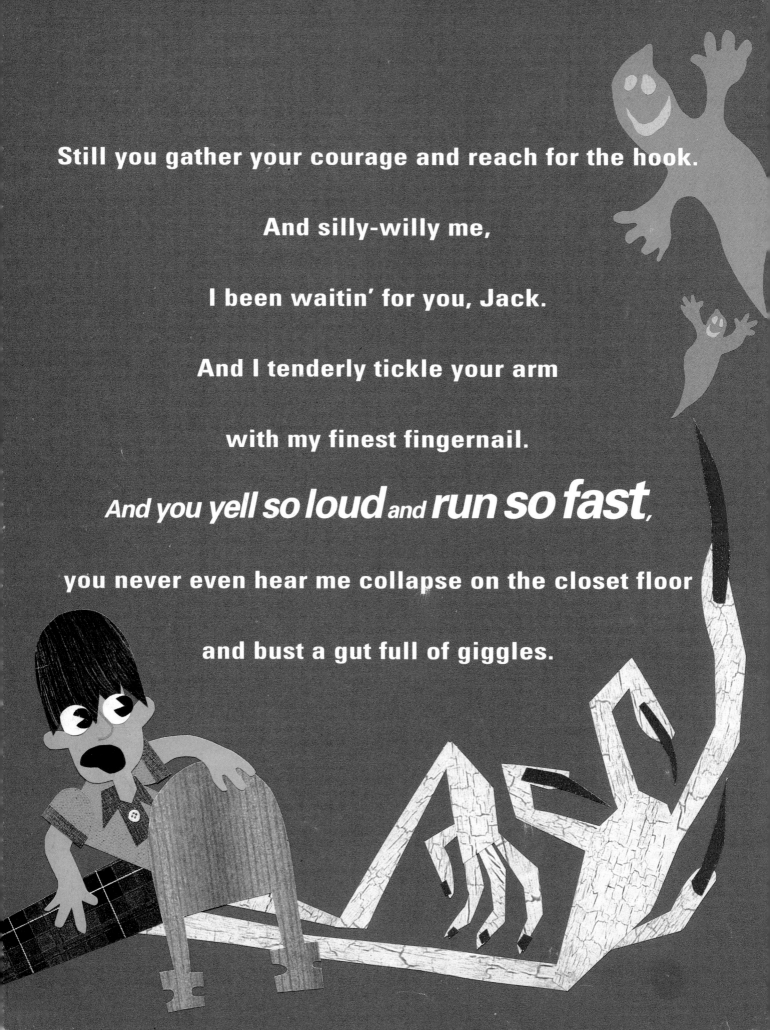

Still you gather your courage and reach for the hook.

And silly-willy me,

I been waitin' for you, Jack.

And I tenderly tickle your arm

with my finest fingernail.

And you *yell so loud* and **run so fast**,

you never even hear me collapse on the closet floor

and bust a gut full of giggles.

I don't

Bellow.

Why, I rarely even raise my voice.

I'm a **professional**, Peppie.

I *whissssssper* and I *murrrmurrr.*

And I *whoooooosh* and *swooooosh* and *saaaail.*

And, weather permitting,

I even *waffffffft* on warm summer winds.

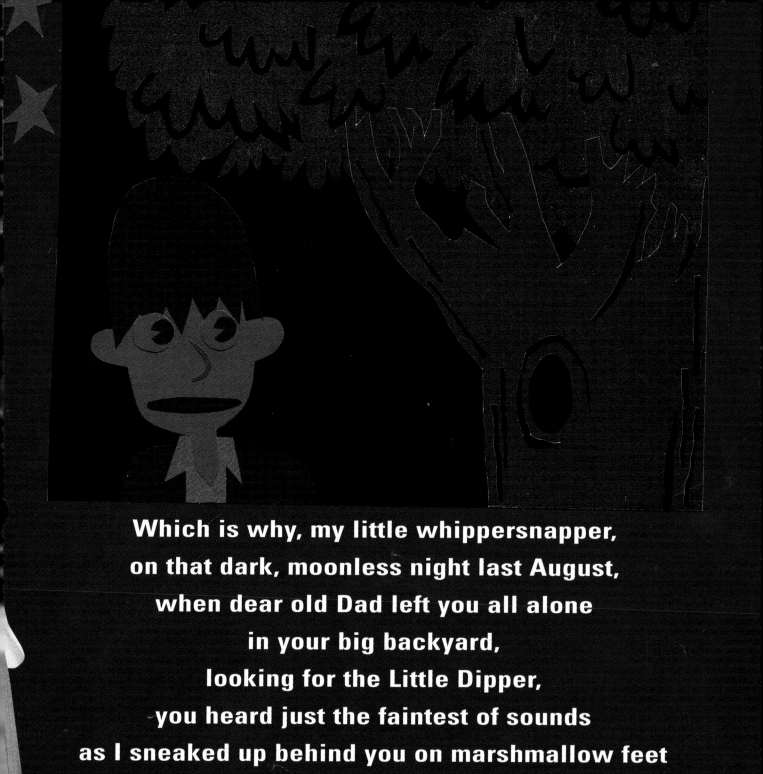

Which is why, my little whippersnapper,
on that dark, moonless night last August,
when dear old Dad left you all alone
in your big backyard,
looking for the Little Dipper,
you heard just the faintest of sounds
as I sneaked up behind you on marshmallow feet
and fluttered my eyelashes close to your ear.

th-then th-th that's when
you s-s-sensed that you (gulp)
w-w-weren't alone,
and the hairs on your neck tried to stand up and run
as your knockin', rockin' legs
turned to jiggle-jam-jelly.
And seriously, Seymour,
don't you just *hate* it when that happens?

NEWS FLASH Number Four:

The Bogeyman does not "GET YA."

What does that even mean, *get ya*?

If I *got ya*,

what would I do *with ya*?

Where would I *put ya*?

And what would I *feed ya*?

My job is to *scare ya*.

I don't want to *raise ya*.

So enough already with the *get ya* garbage.

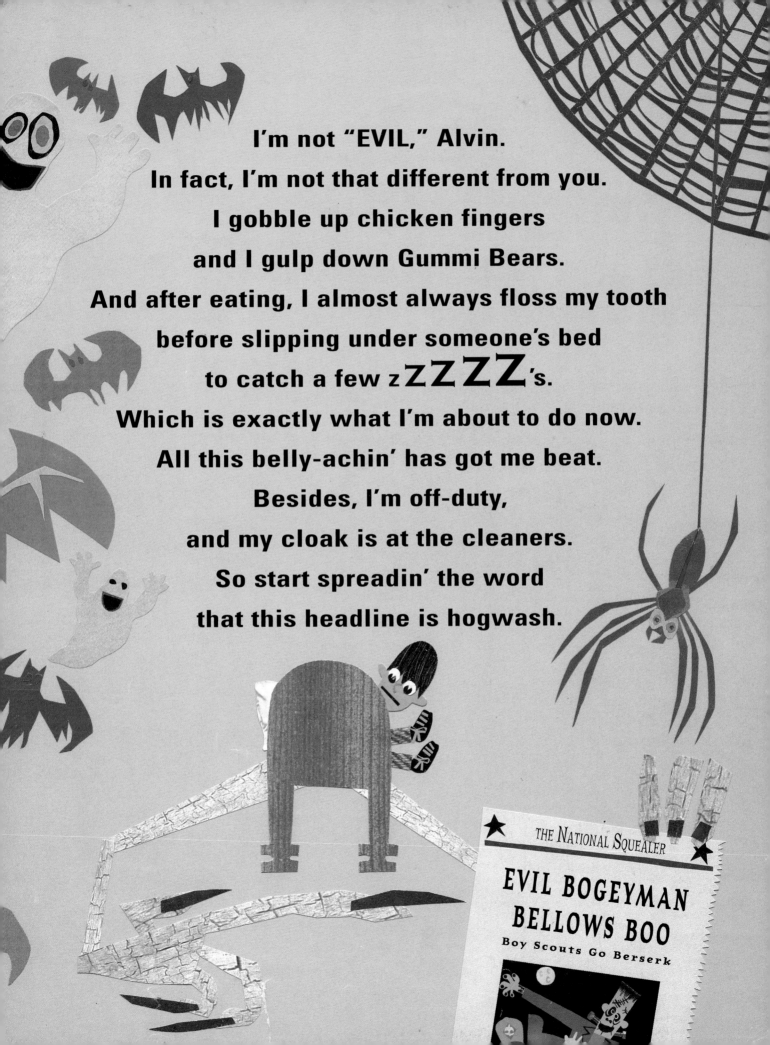

I'm not "EVIL," Alvin.
In fact, I'm not that different from you.
I gobble up chicken fingers
and I gulp down Gummi Bears.
And after eating, I almost always floss my tooth
before slipping under someone's bed
to catch a few z ZZZZ's.
Which is exactly what I'm about to do now.
All this belly-achin' has got me beat.
Besides, I'm off-duty,
and my cloak is at the cleaners.
So start spreadin' the word
that this headline is hogwash.

★ THE NATIONAL SQUEALER

EVIL BOGEYMAN
BELLOWS BOO
Boy Scouts Go Berserk

Oh yeah, and kindly keep your smelly sweatsocks
off the floor.
I'm allergic, okay?
Just one whiff of those things
and I'm outa here, Dude.
I start gaspin' and wheezin' and
chokin' and sneezin'.
Plus I break out in itchy, splotchy blue blotchies.
So like I said, just keep them—

Whoa, whoa, whoa!

Hold on a second, Sherlock.

You're not taking off those socks now, are you?

You are?

But . . . but I thought we were pals.

Hey! Stop waving them around!

What's gotten into you anyway?

Ugh!

Bluck!!!

Ick!

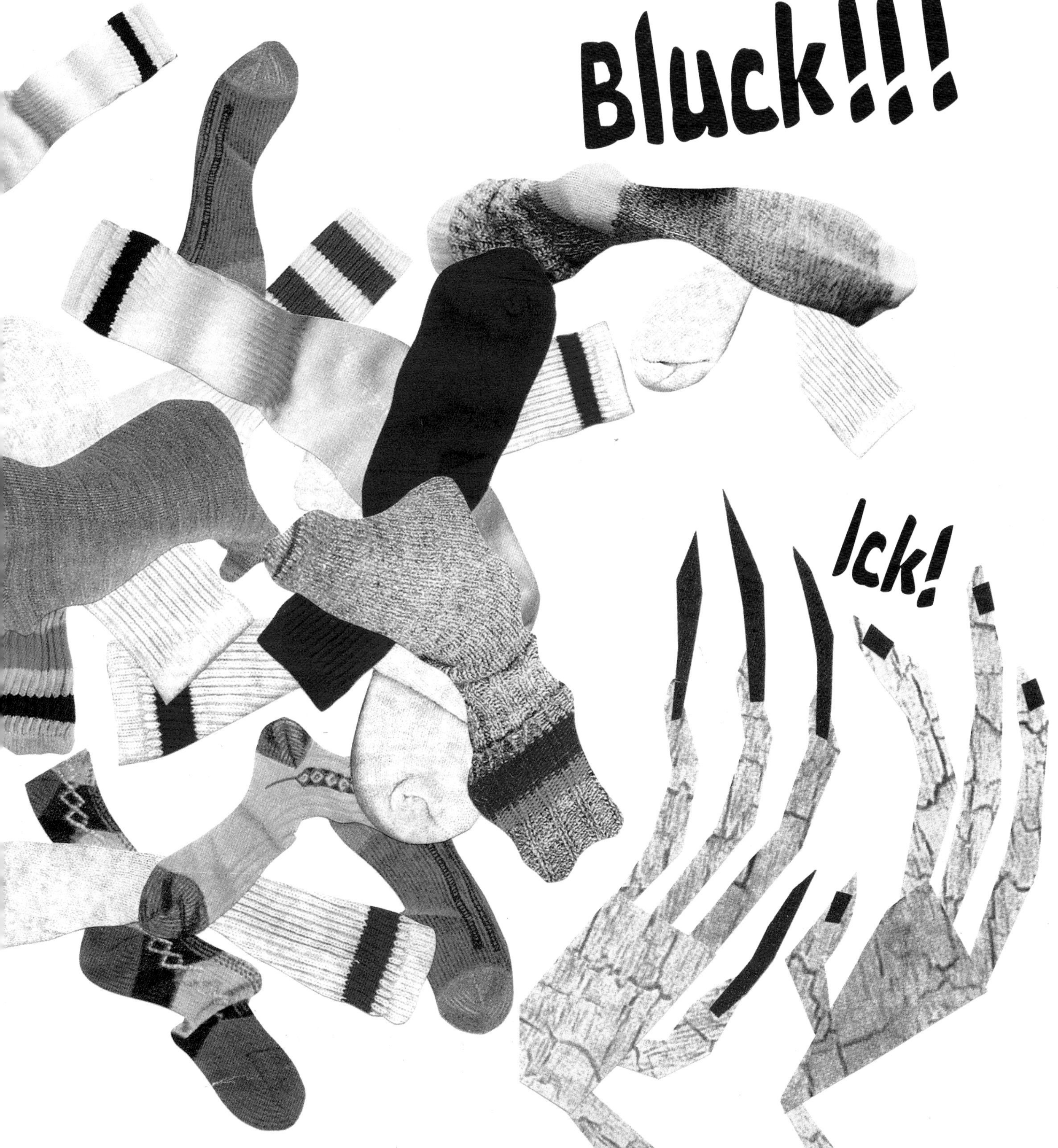

AAAUUUGGGGHH

TO MY SISTER'S ROOM →

THE NATIONAL SQUEALER

★ EVIL BOGEYMAN BELLOWS BOO ★

Boy Scouts Go Berserk

THE BOGEYMAN WILL GET YA IF YA DON'T WATCH OUT

I'm gone!

Pssssssssst!

Yo!

Down here . . . under the bed.

It's *me,*
the Bogeyman.